A Pattern of Murder

by Paul Trembling

Published by Paul Trembling, 2013.

This is a work of fiction. Similarities to real people, places, or events are entirely coincidental.

A PATTERN OF MURDER

First edition. April 23, 2013.

Copyright © 2013 Paul Trembling.

ISBN: 978-1484858127

Written by Paul Trembling.

10 9 8 7 6 5 4 3 2 1

To my colleagues - CSI's, Police Officers, PCSO's and Firefighters.

Only you know the real stories!

A Pattern of Murder.

Ben Drummond didn't like bungalows. He especially didn't like large, sprawling, over-priced bungalows in well-to-do areas, isolated from the rest of the world by their own extensive grounds. Nor did he like the sort of people who lived in them, wealthy people who valued their privacy but were – in Ben's opinion – too bone idle to go upstairs to bed. Hence they had bungalows built for them.

There was no particular reason for this prejudice. Ben collected prejudices the way some people collected stamps, and didn't bother to justify his attitude with reasons. Bungalows and their occupants were just two more facets of his general dissatisfaction with the universe.

He did, however, quite like crime scenes. He especially liked crime scenes in affluent areas, because he liked the idea of the rich and the smug being dragged down to the same sad reality he himself occupied. Plus which, the houses usually smelled better. And – on a purely practical level – it was easier to find forensic evidence in clean and generally tidy houses than in messy ones.

He rang the bell, flashed his ID as it opened, and introduced himself in his usual friendly fashion. "Scenes of Crime Officer. Are you Teller?"

The man at the door nodded. "Yes. Reginald Teller."

"What's happened, then?" Ben asked.

Teller raised an eyebrow. "We've been burgled!" he said, giving Ben a 'don't ask stupid questions' sort of look.

Scenes of Crime Officers are expected to treat members of the public with courtesy and respect. Ben had always found that a bit of a challenge, and Teller wasn't encouraging him in that direction.

"Yes, I know," he answered acerbically. "That's why I'm here. Because *you* reported a burglary." Ben was tempted to ask if Teller often had SOCO's drop in on him just in passing, but he'd had too many warnings lately about his attitude. "I need some more details. Start with when you found it."

"Hmm." Teller looked annoyed. Tall, balding, and sharp featured, he was immaculately if casually dressed and had the air of someone who would take no nonsense. Ben added 'pompous fart' to his assessment. At six foot tall, he matched Teller for size, and could easily outdo him for attitude. Apart from that, they had nothing in common, Ben being unremittingly shabby in appearance, with an untidy shock of iron-grey hair over his fleshy visage. Traces of fingerprint powder on his jacket were, of course, the natural result of his job, but the greasy food stains on his shirt and tie were all Ben.

"You reported it at fourteen hundred." Ben prompted. "That's two o'clock this afternoon," he added patronisingly.

"Yes," Teller conceded reluctantly. "My wife and I had been out all morning. We'd gone in her car." He indicated a silver Lexus parked on the drive next to Ben's SOCO van. "The first thing we noticed was that my Range Rover, which had been left outside the garage, was missing. Then we saw that the front door was ajar, and when we entered there was broken glass in the back bedroom. Glass with blood on it – so that should make your job easier!"

"Maybe." Ben had been a SOCO for more than thirty years. He didn't care for people telling him how to do his job. "Anything else taken apart from the car?"

Teller shook his head. "As far as we can see, the intruder went straight from the bedroom to the kitchen at the front, took the car keys from the drawer where we keep them, and left through the front door."

"No signs of a search?" Ben frowned when Teller confirmed it. "How many people know where you keep your keys?"

"Not many."

Another voice, a women's, broke in on the conversation. "We know exactly who did this – and we've already given his name to the Police!"

"And you are?" asked Ben. The woman had come out of one of the inner rooms, and was peering round Teller's shoulder. Short, thin, and blonde, with a supercilious expression.

"Rosemary Teller," she informed Ben. "We're quite sure that it was Marcus. Marcus Teller, Reginald's brother. An ex-convict, by the way! He's been causing us a lot of trouble lately. Demanding money! When we told him that he had had enough charity from us he turned very nasty and threatened to take what he wanted! And of course, he knew where we kept the keys."

"He knew the alarm code as well," her husband added, seeing Ben glance at the sensor in the hallway.

"What did he need your money for?" Ben enquired. His glance at the alarm sensor, high up on the far wall of the hallway, had shown him something else of interest, but he refrained from looking too closely at it. He was wondering if the Teller's were going to mention it, and didn't want to prompt them.

"Well, how would we know?" Mrs Teller snapped. "Debts? Drugs? Really, we've no idea what he's been up to since he came out of prison! And in any case, I don't see what difference it makes to your investigation! The Police Officer told us that you just needed to take a sample of the blood."

"I'm afraid that there's rather more to it than that, Mrs Teller," Ben said politely. Ben, being polite, would have been a major danger signal to anyone who knew him. The Tellers, however, had not had that dubious privilege. "I was wondering why he only took the car, when he had opportunity to search the entire house and take what he wanted. Was there a specific amount that he was asking for? Perhaps the equivalent in value to your Range Rover?"

3

Observation is an important skill in crime scene examinations, and Ben was very observant. He caught the glance that the Teller's exchanged. Reginald looked alarmed, he thought.

"He'd cut himself, he was bleeding – and he didn't know how soon we'd be back – of course he was in a hurry!" Rosemary said firmly.

"Yes, that may be it." Ben agreed. "Perhaps you'd better show me where this blood is?"

The Teller's led him through the house to a bedroom. Nicely furnished, Ben thought, but with a disused look to it.

"Whose room is this?" he asked.

"It's a guest room," said Reginald. "Marcus stayed here for a while. Just after he was released – we let him live with us until his demands became too impossible!"

A large casement window had been smashed, and there was a considerable quantity of glass on the window sill and floor below. The window was wide open.

"So he smashed the glass, reached in, opened the window and climbed through." Ben summarised. "Were the windows locked?"

There was another swift exchange of glances between the Tellers. "Apparently not," Rosemary admitted grudgingly. "Marcus may have left them unlocked when he was here." She dealt with all the difficult questions, Ben noticed.

"How long ago was that?"

"About a month," said Reginald.

"And you haven't checked them since?"

"An oversight. I thought Reginald had done it."

"A month with insecure windows? You have been living dangerously." Ben said, with a hint of sarcasm. He fished a torch out of one pocket, and a pair of disposable gloves from another. Putting them on, he began a close examination of the glass fragments, several of which were smeared with a dark red substance. Expanding his search, he looked carefully at the carpeted floor, concentrating on the area between the window and the door.

"Well, at least he's spared your carpet. No sign of any drips."

"It was probably just a small cut," Rosemary said quickly. "But there's enough there for identification, I presume?"

Ben nodded. "I'll have to run a test to confirm that it is blood, but yes, there's quite enough."

He stepped past the Teller's, and walked back towards the kitchen, his eyes on the floor. The hallway floor was uncarpeted, floored instead with expensive looking oak boards. About half-way along he stopped and knelt down, shining his torch into the crack between two of them.

"Oh, good," he said brightly. "It looks like we've got some more blood down here!"

He looked along the crack, turned his attention to the neighbouring boards, then looked up at the Tellers.

"Blood in the cracks, but not on the boards. Either our offender was very careful where he dripped – or some bugger's cleaned up!" He shot an accusing glance at the Tellers.

Reginald looked flustered, but Rosemary met his gaze head on. "It was *ruining* the floor!" she said tightly. "And there's plenty of blood on the glass in the bedroom. You said yourself that it was enough!"

Ben indicated the floor boards he had just examined. "We're looking at an area of two or three square feet, Mrs Teller. I'll know for sure later. We'll put a chemical down which will glow nicely where there's any trace of blood. But I don't think that this came from a *small* cut!"

The Tellers were looking at each other again, and at the floor. Which was where Ben wanted them looking, and not at the hallway ceiling.

What Ben had seen there – but the Tellers apparently had not – was the most interesting pattern of blood spots he had come across in many a scene examination. They formed at least two distinct lines, radiating out from a common centre in a rough 'V' shape. The pointy end was almost directly above the pool of blood that

Mrs Teller had so tidily cleaned up. Ben found it amusing that she had been so concerned with the blood on the floor that she hadn't thought to look up and see the much more incriminating blood on the ceiling.

Still, he thought, it would be best to move them out of the hallway. He stood abruptly and went into the kitchen, at the front of the house.

Unsurprisingly, it was large, modern and immaculate. Apart from one draw which was partially pulled out and had a distinct smear of blood across its shiny front.

"That's the draw that the keys were in." Rosemary informed him. "You can see the blood on it – conclusive evidence, I would have thought!" She glared as she spoke, challenging him to dispute the facts.

"And is that the only place he touched, or did you clean up in here as well?" he glared back at her.

She bristled. "I find your tone very objectionable! You should be aware that we regularly play golf with your Chief Constable – and I will be talking to him about this!"

Ben Drummond was not a man to be impressed by mention of the Chief Constable, and he had nothing but derision for golf and anyone who played it. As far as he was concerned, it was a game for people too lazy to run. Not that Ben did much running himself, but then he didn't play games either.

"What's interesting here," he continued - ignoring her threat - "Is all those nice clean tea-towels hanging up over there. If I came in here, bleeding heavily enough to leave a big pool in the hall, I'd have grabbed something to try and stop the bleeding. So are you quite sure that you didn't tidy up in here as well?"

Rosemary looked defiant, Reginald frowned, but neither said anything.

"Right, then. I need to get my camera. This all has to be recorded."

He marched outside, the Tellers in his wake, and headed for his van. Half-way there, he stopped and looked at the big detached double garage.

"Do you normally keep your cars in there?" he asked.

"Yes," said Reginald. "No!" said his wife simultaneously. She gave her husband a fierce look, and turned back to Ben. "Normally we do keep them there," she explained. "At the moment it's full of – of other things. Things in storage. But I don't see how that's relevant!"

Ben shrugged. "Might not be. But if we're looking for a missing vehicle, it might be useful to get some tyre tread marks. Something that shows the wear pattern on the tread. Sort of thing you might find on a garage floor."

That was close to complete bullshit. Tracing cars by tyre tread patterns was not a very reliable technique, but Ben didn't want the Tellers thinking that he had any real interest in the garage. Not just yet, anyhow.

"There aren't any tyre marks in the garage." Mrs Teller said emphatically.

"OK, then." Ben nodded his acceptance and continued his way to the van. Once inside and out of the Tellers sight, he pulled out his mobile phone.

The call was answered almost at once. "Faringham CID. DS Fayden."

"Hello, Fay! It's Ben Drummond. SOCO."

There was a short pause. DS Fayden disliked being called Fay, and hated having to deal with Ben. Ben enjoyed a mental picture of the detective putting his hand over the mouthpiece and saying 'Damn, what does that bastard want."

"Still there, Fay?" Ben prompted.

"That's DS Fayden to you, Drummond!" Ben mentally sneered at the bluster. "What do you want?"

"This job at 'The Lindens' – it's one of yours?"

"The burglary? DC Clay is OIC."

"Well, Fay, you'd better take it off him quick. Because it's not a burglary, and Sticky Clay is too wet behind the ears – and everywhere else – to be Officer In Charge."

"What do you mean, not a burglary? The PC who attended said it was pretty straightforward!"

Ben snorted derisively. "Then he needs a swift kick up the rectum! He's just walked right through a murder scene! Now I suggest you get yourself and Sticky and anyone else you've got dozing in the office down here right now to arrest a Mr and Mrs Teller. You'll also need to search the garage, where you'll find the allegedly stolen Range Rover, and probably the body of the alleged burglar, a Mr Marcus Teller."

"But – we'll need a search warrant."

"Bugger that! Use your imagination, Fay. I've got blood at the scene and a story that doesn't properly account for it! For all we know, the poor sod might still be alive somewhere! That alone gives you ground for searching. Now get your arse down here! I'll stall them as long as I can, but if they realise I've clocked them, they'll make a run for it."

There was a long pause. "Are you sure about this?"

"Of course I'm sure! BPA, mate."

"BPA? Blood Pattern Analysis?"

Ben rolled his eyes. "No, British Police Association! Bungling Police Amateurs! What do you think BPA means?"

There was a very long pause. "You'd damn well better be right about this, Drummond."

"When am I ever wrong? See you soon, Fay!"

Ben finished the call, and spent a pleasant few moments imagining the chaos which he'd just triggered in the CID office. Then he got out the camera kit and made his way leisurely back to the bungalow.

Once there, he took his time. He spent several minutes setting up each shot, playing with the exposure and flash settings to get the best results and taking several pictures of each blood-marked item or surface. He also paused regularly to draw diagrams, take measurements, and test each smear of blood with a chemical kit that turned a satisfying shade of green on every one.

The Tellers watched him with increasing frustration, but to their questions and objections he only replied, brusquely, that he was 'following procedure'. Which he was, though it was a very long time since he'd followed it so precisely.

Working in this meticulous fashion, he took half an hour to finish in the bedroom and move out into the hallway. He was carefully marking out the bloodstained area on the oak boards – using a bit of yellow chalk for the purpose, and enjoying the tight-lipped fury on Rosemary Teller's face – when he heard several cars pull up outside.

"Ah, the cavalry's arrived at last!" He went outside and saw, not only DS Fayden and DC Clay, but a van load of uniformed coppers.

"What – what are they here for?" asked Reginald, who had gone very pale.

"Oh, I think you know," Ben told him. "And I don't think you're going to be playing golf with the Chief Constable anytime soon!"

Just as Ben had predicted, the Range Rover was in the garage, and in it was the body of a male, deceased, with a large hole in the back of his head, and documents in the name of Marcus Teller in his pockets. There was also a complete set of golf clubs, one of them still thickly crusted with blood and hair.

The duty Senior SOCO came out to the scene, as did the Pathologist and a BPA expert, but Ben made it abundantly clear to all that this was his crime scene, never mind what the book said about procedure. So he finished inside the house and moved on to do the garage as well.

It was quite late when he finally got back to the nick. He was delighted to see that the CID office was still buzzing with activity,

Detectives and Support Staff whose plans for the evening had been cancelled, thanks to him. Ben liked to feel he'd made a difference to people's lives.

After handing all the recovered evidence over to the Exhibits Officer, he went to find DS Fayden.

"So then, Fay me old mate," he said loud enough to be heard all over the office. "How's it going, then?"

DS Fayden gave him a look that managed to combine extreme antipathy with grudging respect. "She's refusing to say a word. But he's given us the full story – blaming her for everything, as they usually do. Seems as though there's been bad blood between him and his brother for years. Something to do with a dispute over the inheritance when their parents died. Reggie got the lion's share, Marcus objected, things got nasty. Eventually, Marcus got put away, with his brother and sister-in-law doing everything possible to help him get there. Once he got out, Marcus came looking for compensation. What he got was a golf club in the head."

Ben nodded. "Well, finally a good use for golf clubs," he said, in full knowledge of the fact that Fayden was an avid golfer. "Never did trust people who play that game," he added, for the fun of it.

Fayden frowned, but wisely ignored the remark. "According to Reginald, it was Rosemary who did the actually bludgeoning."

"Yeah, I can imagine. She looked the sort."

"Then they stuffed the body in the car, put it in the garage, and set it up as a burglary. Not a bad idea, actually. They'd planned to take the body and dump it that night, then leave the car somewhere. When we found the car, any traces of Marcus's blood would be explained by the burglary. He'd just disappear, and no one would have cared much anyhow."

"Would have been a good plan if they'd known about Blood Pattern Analysis," Ben said with satisfaction. "I knew straight away that something was wrong. Just smears of blood on some random bits of glass by the Point Of Entry, another smear on the kitchen drawer – and nothing to connect them. No drips on the carpet, no marks on the doors or the walls. But there had been a big pool of blood in the hallway – before they cleaned it up – that was nowhere near the place where he was supposed to have cut himself."

"And then you saw the blood on the ceiling?"

Ben nodded. "That was what really confirmed it for me. Soon as I saw that, I knew we had a murder scene. Serious assault, at least." He flicked through his scene report till he found the page with a rough diagram of the blood pattern on the ceiling. "The photos will show it better, but this told me that someone had been hit hard, several times. The first blow broke the skull, knocked them down. That was probably enough to kill him, but our Rose isn't the sort of girl to leave things to chance! So she hit him again, in about the same place. This time, the weapon – golf club as it happens – lands in the wound, goes deep, and picks up a nice coating of blood and brain tissue. Rosie girl swings it back for another shot, and flicks a nice line of blood spots along the ceiling. And after that, once more for luck, she does it again and puts a second line on there."

"Reginald is saying that he tried to stop her."

Ben snorted. "Braver man than me, then! I wouldn't want to be within a hundred yards of that harridan – especially not when she's armed with a golf club!" He laughed. "Vicious game, golf!"

A Whiff of Homicide.

Ben Drummond was a big man to start with, and over the years he'd added a family sized beer belly to his six foot height and beefy frame. Watching him struggle into a pair of red overalls was not a pretty sight, and Sam Grindley, the Fire Investigation Officer, politely turned his back. Nor was it a quick operation, and the FIO had time for a lengthy conversation with one of the fire crew before Ben finally managed to zip himself in and lumbered over.

He was not known for fastidious cleanliness at the best of times, and Sam – having something of an expert's eye for such things – saw that the Police issue overalls had been to several crime scenes since their last wash. The smears of grey ash had all but obscured the words 'Scenes of Crime' on the breast pocket. Ben's corpulent face, however, was now a brighter red than the overalls from the struggle, and his untidy mass of iron-grey hair matched the stains almost exactly.

"Morning, Ben," Sam greeted him cheerfully. "Nice day for it, don't you think?"

Ben gave him a suspicious look, as if the FIO had offered him a cheap Rolex. "What the hell's nice about it?"

Sam had worked with Ben many times before, and so was expecting this response. He took off his fire helmet, scratched his head through his close-cropped brown hair, and squinted up at the cloud-laden sky.

"Well, it's not raining, at least. Might even get some sunshine later!"

He gave Ben a bright smile. For height, Sam could match Ben, and for looks he far surpassed him, being almost a poster version of a fireman – rugged and muscular, with a pair of twinkling blue eyes to compare to Ben's muddy brown and red-rimmed peepers.

Sam had one thing in common with Ben, however – he enjoyed winding people up. But whereas Bens approach was straightforward rudeness, Sam was much more subtle, and Ben was one of his favourite targets.

"Did we come here to talk about the weather, or what?" Ben grunted. He didn't like firemen much, and especially didn't like Sam Grindley, whom he considered a mouthy prat.

Sam shrugged, and glanced at his colleague. "Ben, here, is the ultimate professional. Never any time for small talk, just straight down to business! Ben – this is Dave Meedan, the Watch Manager in charge of this incident. He'll bring you up to speed on this morning's adventures!"

The Watch Manager gave Ben a wary look. "We got the first call at about five. Man taking his dog out for an early walk on the fields over there" – he waved his hand in the general direction of open land behind the house – "saw the smoke. We were on scene at five twenty, and found the fire well established in a conservatory at the rear. Forced entry to the front door, a team went in. At this point the fire was still confined to the conservatory, and we brought it under control before it got any further. Once we'd got it out, we found one female occupant in the conservatory, badly burned but still alive at that time. Ambulance was on scene, and got her off to hospital, but she was D.O.A. Smoke inhalation."

Ben turned his attention to the house. A solidly built three story dwelling in a Georgian style, it looked expensive but neglected. The wooden window frames needed paint, the ivy was out of control and the front lawn was knee deep.

"She alone here?" he asked.

Sam nodded. "I had a word with the neighbour. Her husband died a few years ago, and she'd been going downhill ever since. Plenty of money – the old man was a director in some big multi-national – but she spent most of it on booze. Apparently she's become a bit of a recluse. The neighbour used to be on good terms, regular social contact and that sort of thing, and he's tried a few times to visit and see how she is. But she wouldn't even open the door to him last time. Practically lives in the conservatory, it seems - drinking, smoking, and watching telly. Sounds your retirement plan, eh, Ben?" he added with a sly grin.

"Sounds like your Mum," Ben snapped back. "Any family?"

"There's a married daughter, who comes over sometimes. The son-in-law used to do a bit of work round the house for her, but neither of them has been seen in a while. The neighbour thinks they've had a falling out.

"We were called in about three month's ago." put in the Fire Officer. "Rubbish fire in the kitchen. It set off the smoke alarm and that same neighbour called us. When we got her, she'd roused herself enough to dump the bin out of the window, and told us to piss off."

"No reports of a smoke alarm this time," Sam added. "Something we'll have to check when we go in."

"Any sign of a forced entry?" Ben wanted to know. "Apart from yours, that is."

Meedan shook his head. "There were windows open in the conservatory, but there's no chance that anyone got in that way. The back is even more overgrown than out here – brambles up to six foot high all along the walls. That's why we had to go in from the front."

"Let's take a look, then." Ben led the way. His nose wrinkled as they opened the front door and the acrid smell reached him.

"Is that the scent of arson, Ben?" Sam asked cheerfully. "Ben's got a good nose for crime scenes," he told Meedan.

The Watch Manager shrugged. "They all smell the same to me. It's worse at the back."

Ignoring them, Ben went through the door. It opened into a wide entrance hall, with a staircase running up on the left and a long corridor on the right, disappearing into the shadowy depths of the house. The only light was from the open doorway, and it faded quickly into a décor of dark wood, heavy floral wall-paper, and paintings of drab landscapes. Ben's attention, however, was mostly on the plastered ceiling, stained black but otherwise appearing unharmed.

"Smoke damage, but not a lot of heat," he commented.

Meedan nodded. "The conservatory door held quite well. The flames were just starting to break through when we got to it."

"And there's the smoke alarm, Ben," Sam added. He switched on his torch and pointed the beam towards the corridor ceiling, just at the point where it entered the hall. "Looks undamaged – so why didn't it go off?"

He walked over to stand below the circle of plastic – once white, now sooty black. Reaching up, he flicked the cover open.

"Someone tampered with it?" Ben asked hopefully. "Wires cut? Battery removed?"

Sam shook his head. "Sorry to disappoint you. It's all intact. Which leaves the question of why it didn't go off?"

"Battery looks a bit old," commented Meedan. "The case is corroded."

"So it is." Sam agreed. Stretching up, he plucked the battery out of its holder, and wiped it clean on the back of his glove before examining it more closely. "I certainly wouldn't trust my life on this one. But let's make sure." Pulling a battery tester from one of his pockets, he clipped the suspect item into the terminals and examined the dial. "Flat as the proverbial pancake. So that's one mystery solved, eh Ben?" He gave the SOCO a bright smile.

"Is it heck!" Ben snapped. "It was working fine the last time you came! Why not now?"

"Three months, Ben. Three months in neglected house, and I doubt if it was tested regularly. Three months is plenty of time for a battery to fail under those conditions."

Ben took the offending item off Sam, and glared at it. "Looks like more than three months old to me," he muttered, and slipped it into an evidence bag. "I'll send it off to the lab, see if they can get anything."

"We don't know how long it had been there before." Sam pointed out. "But if you want it, Ben, you take it!"

The smell of wet, charred wood grew stronger as they went down the corridor. It ended in a sharp right turn, and opened out into a cluttered lounge. The wooden door was held open by a worn-looking leather armchair. The rest of the room was similarly furnished – all dark wood and leather, no doubt expensive when new, but now looking old and shabby. The layer of soot on every surface didn't help, either.

"This is how we found it." Meedan explained. He indicated doorways on either side of the room. "Bathroom over there, kitchen opposite. Doors all wedged open."

"The lady didn't like closed doors." mused Ben. "But the conservatory door was shut?"

"Shut and locked. We had to force it." He pointed to the far end of the room to where a double door of wood and glass hung open, panes shattered and wood splintered.

Sam noticed the gleam of interest in Ben's eyes. "Ah, now you've made Ben a happy man! He does love a locked door mystery! Was she locked inside, Dave?"

"Locked herself in," said Meedan. "We found the key on the floor, inside the conservatory."

"Oh, that's harsh! To ruin a man's dreams with an awkward fact!" Sam gave Ben a gentle nudge in the ribs.

"Sod off." Ben grunted, and picked his way through the furniture towards the conservatory door.

As conservatories went, this had been a big one, about fifteen feet square, Ben judged. Once it would have been a bright, airy space. Now, however, the weak November daylight struggled to force its way through the smoke-blackened glass. The gloom was only relieved by the wide space in the centre of the ceiling, where the panes had cracked and fallen in the heat.

Below, the rest of the room was a confusing jumble of blackened shapes. Plastic had melted, wood had charred, glass had fallen on top and everything was sodden from the fireman's hoses. The reek of it filled their nostrils.

They stood and looked in silence for a few moments, experience enabling them to make sense out of the chaos. Sam pointed his torch upwards, to where the wooden roof beams had burned away entirely.

"Hottest point there, I'd say." He shone the light on the point directly below. "Which would suggest that the main seat of the fire was there." He picked his way through the rubble, knelt at the place he'd indicated, and gently sifted through the debris. "Springs," he commented. "Badly deformed, so subject to a lot of heat. Looks like it could have been a sofa." He shifted position. "And here we've got what's left of some bottles."

Standing up again, he turned and inspected a mass of melted plastic at one side of the conservatory.

"That used to be the TV. So here's a scenario for you, Ben. The lady was sitting here, on the sofa, watching TV, drinking and smoking. She falls asleep, drops her cigarette. It burns its way into the upholstery, and spreads rapidly. The heat goes straight up at first, so you get a hot spot in the ceiling, burning through the wooden beams. It spreads out, and works its way down – see the damage to the window ledge? Deep charring on top, but under the lip it's mostly untouched."

"So you're saying accidental ignition?" Ben frowned. Sam's diagnoses was accurate, and his conclusion logical. It was exactly what Ben would have said if Sam hadn't said it first.

Sam shrugged. "She was alone in a locked room with no other point of entry. Of course, it might not a have been a cigarette, that's just the most likely explanation."

"I did wonder about an electrical fault," Meedan suggested.

"OK, let's look at that." Sam went over to the remains of the TV. Reaching into the ashes he gently teased out a strand of wire, the copper bright against the multiple shades of black that dominated the room. "Insulation all burnt off, but you can still see that it runs back towards the house wall." He followed it along. "Ah, here's the socket. Two gang. Another wire..." he tugged more wire out of the ash "... that goes over there."

Ben sifted through the debris in the direction indicated, and uncovered a small metal box. "Small fan heater. Down by the sofa." He poked at the casing, shone his torch through the grill at the front. "Looks undamaged inside. Didn't start here."

Sam nodded. "And the plugs have melted down from the top, which is consistent with my scenario."

"Where did you find the key?" Ben asked.

"It was underneath the lady when we moved her. Just by the door. Should still be there, actually. We didn't move it."

"You're not back on the Locked Room Mystery, are you Ben?" Sam asked with amusement.

"Doesn't make sense that she propped all the other doors open but locked this one," Ben pointed out.

There was a relatively clear patch of floor next to the door, marking the spot where the woman's body had been. Ben searched around it, and extracted a brass key from under a pile of shattered glass. "Looks like it got kicked out of the way. Don't your people know anything about preserving a scene?"

"They've got their own priorities!" Sam answered firmly. "Like trying to save lives and putting the fire out!"

Ben, having no immediate answer, scowled, and concentrated on examining the key. "Lot of scratches on it," he grunted.

"Keys often have scratches on them."

"Looks like some sort of tool mark." Ben held the key up. "Round the tip, see? I've seen that before. Old burglars trick. If you leave your key in the lock – this sort of lock – they can reach in with some needle-nosed pliers and turn it. That's to get in, of course. But you could do the same thing to lock it from outside!"

Sam considered it. "Nice idea, Ben. But that's reading a lot into a few scratches. More likely, she'd locked it herself. When the flames woke her up, she ran for the door. Fumbled for the key – might have been in her pocket. But she's half-drunk, half-asleep, confused and frightened. She can't manage to get the key in the door, drops it, and is overcome by the smoke before she can find it again." He shook his head. "Not a nice way to go."

Ben shook his head. "I'm not convinced" he said truculently, putting the key back on the floor. "Let's get the sniffer dog out here, and check for accelerants."

Sam sighed. "That's going to take a while, Ben. Mike Warren and his dog are on a job at the other end of the county just now. Are you sure it's necessary?"

"Just get him over here, ASAP!"

"OK, if you insist. But I can tell you now, there's nothing suspicious about this."

Ben didn't really think so either. He couldn't be sure that the scratches on the key were from pliers, and Sam's scenario was realistic. But he certainly wasn't going to give the FIO the satisfaction of knowing that, and if all he could do was to keep everyone hanging around for an unnecessary hour, well, he was up for it.

"I'll get my camera and start recording this lot." He gave them a menacing stare. "Don't touch that key! I don't want it losing again. Oh – and one thing – did you say that there was more than one call?"

"Yes. Second call came in about ten minutes after the first. We were already well on the way then, of course. The caller didn't give a name, and when they were told that we were already responding, they hung up."

"Did it come from a mobile? Was there a number?"

Meedan shook his head. "Call box. The one at the end of the lane, actually – so not far away. Control told us to look out for someone there, thought they might be waiting to guide us in, but it was empty when we went past."

Ben scratched his chin thoughtfully, leaving black smears from the wet ash over his stubble. Sam suppressed a grin. "Where are you going with that one, Ben?" he asked. "Nothing suspicious about a phone call, surely?"

"Why a phone box? And why not wait for you to arrive?"

"Not everyone has a mobile, even nowadays. And perhaps they just didn't want to get involved. Some people are like that."

"So what are they doing down there at that time of the morning anyway?"

"Another dog walker, perhaps?"

"Hell of a lot of dog walkers wandering round here!"

Sam chuckled. "Definite grounds for suspicion, I'd say! But tell me this, Ben – assuming it is connected – why would anyone want to start a fire and then call us to put it out?"

"Someone who wanted to get rid of the old lady but keep the house!" Ben said curtly, and stomped off.

Once outside, he didn't go straight back to his van, but instead walked over the PC controlling the cordon.

"Get on to Control," he told him. "We've got another scene. Phone box at the end of the lane. I want it cordoned and secure, ASAP."

The constable gave him a wary look. "Sergeant won't like that. We're already short-handed. He's been asking if I can be released."

"His problem. Get it done! I'll be down there as soon as I've finished here – but I don't want anyone in or even near that phone box until then! Got that?"

"I'll pass the message. Can't promise anything, though."

"I can promise some arses kicked if it isn't done!" Ben growled. He trudged over to his van, where he got out his camera and a pork pie, and wandered back to the house, chewing and thinking deeply.

In the end, it was nearly two hours before Ben arrived at the telephone box, the sniffer dog having meanwhile arrived, sniffed, wagged its tail and left, without finding anything of interest. Sam, looking as though he would be wagging his tail if he had one, had commiserated insincerely, and also left to write up a report of accidental ignition, possibly through smoking materials.

It was no more than Ben had expected, and he took it out on the young female PCSO guarding the phone box.

"Anybody used that phone box?" he said, glaring.

"No – nobody's even tried to," she replied nervously. "I've only been here an hour, though. They didn't have an officer available before then."

"Wonderful! We've got a scene linked to a potential murder, and it takes an hour to get it preserved!"

She shrugged helplessly. "You'll have to talk to my Sergeant about that."

"I will!" Ben gave her another glare, but in truth he wasn't in a strong position for making complaints. His grounds for demanding a second scene to be put on were tenuous at best, and the chances of finding anything of evidential value in a public telephone box were slim. It wasn't the preservation issue that really annoyed him though – it was the prospect of Sam Grindley being right.

He put on a fresh set of disposable gloves, and began his examination. It took perhaps thirty seconds to confirm his expectations. The glass panes of the box were scuffed and dirty. The plastic handset itself was worn and cracked by long and careless usage, and the concrete floor was littered with crushed cigarette ends and assorted rubbish. Graffiti was scrawled over all possible surfaces, most of it both obscene and badly spelt.

With a sigh, Ben got out his brush and dusted the handset lightly with aluminium powder. Nothing developed apart from a few vaguely finger-shaped marks and a lot more scratches. He took some small satisfaction from the thought that the next person to use it would get shiny powder stains on their hands and ear – but however good it was as a practical joke, forensically it was useless.

He stepped outside again.

"Get anything?" asked the PCSO.

He glowered. "I'm still looking!"

He made a pretence of examining the ground around the telephone box, but the rough tarmac had no secrets to hide. He poked around in the hedge behind, and dislodged several ancient beer cans.

"Dunno why they stuff their rubbish in the hedge, when there's a rubbish bin just there!" The PCSO commented. Trying to build bridges with Ben, which was a waste of time, but she hadn't met him before.

"Why take two steps over to the rubbish bin when you've got a perfectly good hedge right next to you!" he retorted.

"That's a terrible attitude to take!" she replied. Defensive, but not easily brow-beaten. "Rubbish put in hedges just stays there! If it goes in the bin, you know that it's going to be disposed off."

Ben opened his mouth to make a withering response, then stopped, and mentally kicked himself. "That's right," he told her. "Which is why I need to examine the bin as well. Can I assume that it hasn't been used?"

"Not while I've been here."

The Police Crime Scene tape had actually been tied around the rubbish bin, so technically it was inside the cordon. Ben gently lifted the metal flap on top, and shone his torch inside.

The PCSO didn't know it, but the sight she was then treated to was one of the rarest in the annals of Police history – Ben Drummond, with a wide smile spreading across his podgy features.

"Tell me, officer," he asked. "Why would someone come out here to dump a pair of rubber gloves?"

"Well – perhaps a dog walker, cleaning up the mess?"

"Dog walkers again!" Ben snorted. "Who uses a pair of brand new kitchen gloves for picking up dog crap? And in any case, there's no smelly brown stuff on them."

She shrugged. "Then I've no idea."

"Well I have. I have a very good idea!" He fetched his camera, and while the PCSO held the flap open, carefully photographed the gloves before lifting them out and bagging them up.

His grin turned almost beatific when he saw the shiny new battery that had been underneath the gloves.

It was some three weeks later when Ben received a phone call from Sam Grindley. It was a call he had been anticipating with relish.

"I hear that they've arrested someone for that conservatory fire," the FIO began.

"Yeah. The son-in-law."

"So how did you get onto him?"

"DNA from his gloves," Ben explained. "Nice, warm, sweaty rubber gloves, which he'd bought especially for the purpose, so there was no chance of a mixed profile from other users." He went on to explain in some detail how, where and why the gloves had been found.

"So he'd gone in the house when he knew the old lady was probably asleep in the conservatory," Sam summarised. "Changed the smoke alarm battery. Dropped a cigarette end on the sofa, used that trick you talked about to lock the door, then went down to the phone box and called it in when the fire was well established."

"That's it," Ben confirmed. "He wanted rid of the old lady, but he wanted the house! With her gone, him and his wife stood to inherit the lot. Bit of a shock when he found out that your lads were already on their way! I reckon he panicked a bit – didn't want the battery and the gloves on him, so he dumped them in the nearest bin!"

"Not that strong a case, though," Sam pointed out. "Doesn't directly tie him in to the fire."

"No, but it gave CID some good questions to ask, and he gave the wrong answers! Tried to make out that he'd put the gloves in there weeks ago, but even our Council gets round to emptying the bins more often than that! He also said that he was out of town when it happened, but CCTV picked up his car going through the town centre at about four that morning. And also coming back again at half-past five. Which, by the way, his wife hadn't known about! She was devastated by what happened to her mother – when she found out what he'd been up to she went ballistic. Would have killed him herself if she could have got to him! Apparently, he's been running up a lot of debt, and getting more and more pissed off with the old lady for drinking away the money! In any case, he's coughed to it now. He's saying that he just trying to give her a scare, so that she'd agree to going into a home."

"Locking someone in a burning room – that's pretty scary," Sam agreed.

"Ah, yes – regarding that locked room," Ben continued with enthusiasm. "We found a pair of needle-nosed pliers in his car. They've gone off to the lab, along with the key, to see if they can match the marks."

"Looks like you've got him, then."

"Absolutely. Bang to rights!" Ben was enjoying himself hugely. "And you wrote it up as an accident!"

There was a long pause.

"Well, Ben, I've got to hand it to you – you were right and I was wrong! Congratulations mate. Stunning job!"

Ben swore, and slammed the phone down, his good mood ruined. He hated a good loser. It took all the fun out of winning.

A Step Too Close To Death.

Ben Drummond would not have been called a fanciful man by anyone who knew him. But he had his daydreams, all the same. Privately, he considered that he had been born into the wrong place and the wrong time. His true calling was to be a Private Eye in 1930's USA: and in quiet moments, that was where he liked to go.

One of those moments found him in the Scenes of Crime Office at Ash Hill Police Station. He was settled comfortably in a large and non-regulation chair, with his feet up on a desk, a packet of chocolate digestives at hand and a mug of tea resting on his ample stomach. It was a quiet day. Quiet for him, that was. There had been the usual smattering of burglaries, criminal damage incidents and 'Theft From Motor Vehicle's, but nothing that grabbed his interest. The other SOCO's could deal with the minor stuff. Ben, with nearly thirty years experience behind him, wasn't about to move out of the office for anything less than an aggravated burglary.

So he closed his eyes and slipped into his other persona, 'Slick' Drummond, relaxing in his New York office with a glass of bourbon, reading the newspaper report of his latest triumph.

Then there'd be a knock on the door, and in would come a tall, shapely blonde. A real looker, except that her eyes were red with grief.

"Please, Mr Drummond,' she'd say. "You've just gotta help me! I've got no one else to turn to!"

And he'd tilt back his hat; give her a long look, then say...

"Siddown, doll, and tell me all about it."

"WHAT DID YOU JUST CALL ME?"

The angry voice broke abruptly into Ben's pleasant little fantasy, causing him to jerk upright and spill hot tea over his shirt.

"Ouch!" He turned, glaring, to meet the equally furious gaze of DI Helen Wheeler. Head of Ash Hill CID's Major Incident Unit, and sometimes referred to (quietly) as 'Hel on Wheels' for the furious drive and energy she displayed on major crime investigations. She was not known to put up with anything resembling disrespect.

Anyone else would have blushed and apologised profusely. Ben, whose instinct for antagonism bordered on the suicidal, instead chose the road of confrontation.

"You made me spill my tea!" he accused, mopping ineffectually at his freshly stained shirt with a handkerchief, itself bearing many stains of much older provenance. "You could have scalded me!"

Unlike some, DI Wheeler was not in the least intimidated by Ben's bluster. She met him eye for eye.

Though not the woman of Ben's daydream, Helen Wheeler was at least blonde, and not unattractive, with regular features on a round face, beneath short cropped hair, and with a lean and athletic – if hardly voluptuous – figure. She was clothed in a business-like dark suit, and those who happened to have met her socially reported that she scrubbed up very nicely.

Which wasn't something anyone had ever said about Ben, whose unruly mop of grey hair was clearly not in any sort of relationship with a comb. His face, like the rest of him, tended more towards general bulkiness rather than any particular shape, and his grubby clothing had very probably been slept in more than once.

The only thing the two had in common was attitude. Ben, for his part, had no intention of being talked down to by a woman who he remembered as a snotty young recruit. DI Wheeler, however, was unimpressed by his experience, his ugliness or his belligerence.

She did, however, have more important things to do. Putting Ben Drummond in his place was something she could attend to at a later date.

"Get your kit together, Drummond. We've got a fatality, potential murder. It's an outside scene and the weather outlook is poor. I'm on my way there now. I want you no more than ten minutes behind me – is that clear?"

Ben frowned. "The duty Senior SOCO..."

"Is at a Post Mortem, and won't be free for two or three hours. We can't wait that long. I've already spoken to him. You're the only SOCO available, Drummond...' she paused there for a moment, the unspoken words 'heaven help us' hanging between them "...so get yourself moving. It's in the patch of woodland behind Balaclava Street. Do you know it?"

"Of course!" said Ben, indignantly. He prided himself on his knowledge of the area, and Balaclava Street was a regular stop for all Ash Hill officers. It had been appropriate to name it after a battle, since it was one of the most unruly and crime-ridden parts of the city.

"Good. I'll brief you at the scene. Oh, and in future, Drummond – you address me as Detective Inspector Wheeler, or Ma'am!" She turned and left as abruptly as she'd arrived.

Ben stared moodily after her. He'd day-dreamed of a blonde who came asking for his help. Instead he got Hel on Wheels, demanding his attendance. Life somehow never lived up to his expectations.

Still, he thought, brightening up a bit, at least the job might be interesting. Even Balaclava Street didn't get a murder every day.

Despite his excess poundage, Ben could move fast enough when he wanted to, and – slightly to her surprise – the DI had only been at the scene for five minutes herself, when Ben came stomping down the muddy path that led off the end of the street. He had squeezed himself into a white forensic suit (size extra large) and was laden down with fingerprint kit and camera bag. He had commandeered a Constable to carry the tripod and other equipment.

The path led down a thirty degree slope through a scrappy bit of woodland left over from the days before the city had absorbed the surrounding farmlands. At the bottom of the slope the path turned right, running along the edge of a five foot deep ditch half full of stagnant water and eventually coming out behind "The Hussar', a local pub known for flat beer, stale sandwiches and good drugs.

There was a paramedics blanket on the side of the path, draped over a human shaped object. Ben put his gear down, wandered over and pulled away the covering.

"Sad business," said the Constable.

Ben grunted. He'd seen too many bodies in his time to feel any emotion about this one. Many Police Officers and SOCO's put on an armour of practiced cynicism to protect themselves against the overload of human tragedy. Ben had been wearing his so long that it had sunk into his soul.

"How many happy corpses have you seen, then?" he asked.

The DI, who had been conferring with some of her team, came over and joined them. "Thank you, Williams," she said to the Constable. "You can get back on the cordon now. As long as Mr. Drummond has finished with you?" she added, pointedly. "After all, preserving the scene isn't a priority, is it?"

"You wanted me to hurry," Ben muttered, without interrupting his study.

She had been a tiny little thing, he thought. Probably not much over five foot high when she was standing, and skinny with it. Her pink gilet was streaked with mud and opened out, the red t-shirt beneath had been pulled up to enable the paramedics to do their work. She had black jeans, pink and white trainers, and short blonde hair with dark roots showing through. Her eyes stared uncaring up at the menacingly dark clouds that stooped over them.

"Her names Kaylie Cobden," Wheeler informed him. "Twenty two years old."

"Where was she found?"

"About here, but we think she'd fallen into the ditch. Or been pushed."

"Drowned?" Ben glanced down at the brackish water. There was no telling how deep it went.

"Broken neck, the Paramedics think. It'll go to Post Mortem, of course."

"So what's the story?"

"She lived up on Balaclava Street with her boyfriend, Gary Mark Branden. Gazza to his friends. According to him – and we don't have any other witnesses as yet – they came out of their flat at about sixteen-thirty. They were going to get a takeaway from the curry house the other side of the pub. He says that they'd had a bit of a fight, exchanged some words, and he'd gone off ahead of her. He'd just got to the bottom of the hill and was walking along this section, when someone hit him from behind. He doesn't remember much else for a bit, but when he came round, she was laying face-down in the bottom of the ditch. He went down the bank, dragged her out, but couldn't get any response. Since he didn't have his mobile on him, he ran to the pub and phoned the ambulance from there."

"Any sign of this mysterious attacker?"

Williams shook her head. "We've checked CCTV at the pub. They've got a camera that covers the car park and the end of the path, but in that time frame the only person to come that way was Branden. What's more, no one else went up the path from that direction either. The alleged assailant could have been there already and have gone back up the bank onto Balaclava Street, of course. We're still doing house-to-house along there. So far, three people have confirmed seeing Cobden and Branden go down the path – and confirmed that they were arguing – but no one else was seen going that way, or coming from that direction."

Ben scratched his chin. "Well, you could go along the ditch, and then climb out at the bridge on Mill Lane. But it would be hard going, with all the brambles and nettles."

"It's been checked. It would have been easy to spot if someone had forced their way through the undergrowth, but there's no sign of that. The other end of the ditch has been looked at as well, but it disappears into a culvert under the dual-carriageway. Undamaged steel grid over the entrance, and sheer concrete walls either side. No one went that way."

"The story sounds a bit thin, then."

The DI nodded. "And what's more, Branden's got form for assault. Especially on women. He likes to drink, and when he's drunk, he likes to use his fists. He's knocked several of his girlfriends about in the past. The last one he put into hospital. He went down for that, and only got out a couple of years ago."

"So he's well in the frame for this one, then. Any trouble since he came out?"

"Ah, now that's interesting. He met up with Cobden shortly after his release, and she seemed to have had a good influence on him. He's been as good as gold – not even a 'drunk and disorderly'. And their relationship has been quite stable, by all accounts."

"Until today's argument."

She shrugged. "What we're hearing from the neighbours is that they argued all the time! Apparently, she had a temper even worse than his, and without needing to be drunk! The couple in the flat below said it was always her voice they heard screaming obscenities, and she regularly used to throw things at him."

"And that's a stable relationship?"

"It seemed to work for them. At least, she'd kept him off the booze and out of trouble – and there's no reports that he's every laid a finger on her. Before today, that is."

"So what changed? Had he finally had enough of her?"

"Perhaps. But I'm wondering if he hadn't started drinking again. That could have been what they were arguing about." She pointed towards an empty bottle laying beside the path. "So I'm particularly interested in that, Drummond. I want it photographing, swabbing and fingerprinting as a priority."

"Why that one especially?" Ben waved an arm at the bushes behind him. "This little bit of nature is also the local rubbish dump. There are more bottles and cans littering this place than there are on the pub premises!"

DI Wheeler gave him a grim smile. "I know. And I expect you to examine them as well! But that one is the closest to where the incident occurred."

Ben looked at the bottle with distaste. "So you're suggesting that he'd had a few drinks, she tried to stop him, and he hit her. Knocked her into the ditch and broke her neck. When he realised what he'd done, he calls the ambulance and makes up this story about being hit from behind."

"That's one possible scenario. I'm keeping an open mind, of course. I'm hoping you'll give me something conclusive. Branden's DNA or fingerprints on the bottle would be useful."

"And does he have any injuries to back up his story?"

Wheeler frowned. "Yes. He has a wound on the back of the head. It would be consistent with being struck from behind, and was hard enough to break the skin. He had a lot of blood over his back and shoulders. It could have stunned him, possibly rendered him unconscious."

"Oh, dear," said Ben solicitously. "That doesn't fit our scenario at all."

"We don't know that it happened when he said," she answered shortly. "He could have done it afterwards to support his story."

Ben raised an eyebrow. "Really? It's not that easy to hit yourself over the back of the head."

"He could have got someone to do it for him."

Ben shrugged. "Maybe. There are plenty of people on Balaclava who'd happily smack anyone, just as a favour. But it won't be easy to prove."

"Yes, thank you Drummond. I do realise that!" She took a deep breath. "So we need get any forensics we can on whoever's used this footpath in the last few hours. Fortunately, this isn't a proper public right-of-way. It's only used by locals."

"The entire population of Balaclava Street!" Ben snorted.

"It's a manageable number," she answered briskly. "My team is going to start going along the street, checking every bit of footwear owned by every member of every household and they will take possession of every item with the slightest trace of mud visible. Or any that look like they've been washed recently. Your part, Drummond, is to record and photograph every footprint along the length of this path!"

He looked at her aghast. "You're bloody joking! There must be hundreds of marks in this mud! And half of them will be from coppers!"

"You can eliminate any that are definitely made by Police Officers. But Branden was wearing a pair of work boots, so take that into account. I want any mark that he might have left, no matter how partial."

He shook his head. "This could take hours! It'll be pitch black along here by then!"

"Not to worry. I'll arrange for some lighting."

"It could start raining at any minute!"

"Then you'd better get a move on, hadn't you? I'm going to set the footwear search in motion, before I nip back to the station to see how the interview with Branden's going. Call up as soon as you get the initial scene photographs done and we'll get the body taken off for Post Mortem. I'll be back here to check on your progress in an hour!"

Ben watched her departing back with incredulity. "They don't call her 'Hel on Wheels' for nothing," he muttered to himself. Some DI's would prefer to stay in the office and run things from there, but Helen Wheeler had a more hands-on approach. It didn't make her popular, but it got results.

Ben turned his attention to the footprints. He was pretty sure that most of the ones in the area were from either Police or paramedics – and regardless of what DI Wheeler wanted, he wasn't going to waste time on marks which were overlaid, or which showed no tread pattern.

That still left a huge number to be considered. But one in particular had caught his eye. In fact he'd noticed it even before the conversation with Wheeler, and now he got out his strongest torch and bent down to give it detailed examination.

What had interested him in the first place was that it was clearly a lot smaller than the majority of marks in the area. It was recent as well, the tread pattern still very sharp and clear – a series of wavy lines and circles. The same pattern, in fact, that he had already noticed on Kaylie Cobden's trainers.

The powerful light, however, revealed something else – a slight discolouration in some of the mud within the mark.

Ben allowed himself a faint smile. Humming tunelessly, he set up the camera and tripod and got to work.

DI Wheeler was exactly on time. One hour to the minute after her departure, she was back at the scene. In the meantime, the clouds had lowered even further, and the light was rapidly fading. Ben's white forensic suit, however, stood out clearly in the murk, and a frown crossed her face when she saw that he was in almost exactly the same place that she'd left him.

"I've got a lighting rig on its way, and we're searching all over the county for enough forensic tents to cover the path."

"No need to bother, Detective Inspector Wheeler Ma'am," Ben replied unctuously. "I'm nearly finished here."

He had a bottle in his hands, and was carefully dusting it with a fingerprint brush, his movements surprisingly delicate for a man of his size and personality. Looking at it, DI Wheeler recognised that it was, in fact, the bottle that she'd pointed out earlier.

33

"So you photographed all the footprints?"

"All the ones that are relevant, Ma'am."

She folder her arms and gave him a hard stare. "You'd better explain that, Drummond, and it had better be a good explanation as well!"

He nodded. "Certainly, Ma'am." He indicated along the path with his torch, where a series of numbered yellow markers stood out in the increasing gloom. "Numbers one to four are prints, or partial prints, of some sort of heavy boot. Not police or paramedic and quite fresh, so I think that they're Branden's. Numbers five, six and seven are smaller. Trainer marks that match Cobden's shoes." He nodded to where the body had been, the undertakers having arrived in the meantime. "We'll have to get them off to the lab for the experts to check, of course."

Wheeler nodded, and Ben continued. "Here's the boot prints again, markers eight and nine, but we've only got the toe end visible. Which would be consistent with someone leaning – or falling – forwards. And there are some deep impressions in the mud just beyond them – ten, eleven, twelve and thirteen – which aren't the right shape at all for shoes or boots. I'm suggesting that those were caused by Branden's hands and knees as he fell forward."

"So you're supporting his story?" she asked evenly.

"Yes, Ma'am – but there's more. Marker fourteen – another one of Cobden's trainer marks, but as you see its right next to the impression possibly left by Branden's hand. And in it I've found traces of blood."

She raised an eyebrow. "Branden's blood, you mean?"

"I think so, Ma'am. We'll have to wait for the DNA test to confirm it, but it seems consistent with the scene. If he was struck from behind, and fell over here – bleeding heavily – then his blood would have been likely to drop in this area."

"And if she came and stood in it, then he couldn't have received the injury afterwards. It confirms his story."

"I tested the soles of her shoes as well, before they took the body," Ben continued. "It's well mixed in with the mud, but I got a positive result for blood. I've taken samples, of course, but we'd best get the shoes themselves sent up to the DNA lab."

"Very well. Good work, Drummond," she said, with only a faint trace of reluctance. "But you still need to record all the other footwear marks. If Branden's story is confirmed, we now have to identify the person who hit him."

"I know who hit him," Ben told her smugly.

"What? Who?"

"Kaylie Cobden."

"Cobden!" Wheeler raised her eyebrows. "OK, lets hear it, then – what makes you think it was her?"

He held up the bottle. "This has been lying around for a while. Look at the water damage on the label? It last rained two days ago, so I'm thinking that it's been here at least that long. Shouldn't be any viable prints left after that amount of time out in the weather. But look what I've just developed along the side there? A full set of fingers! Very fresh, lots of detail – and very small as well. Have to let the Fingerprint Experts check them, of course, but I'll put money on them being Cobden's. There are also traces of blood on the bottle, and that's probably Branden's."

"So when they had their argument, Cobden picked the bottle up from the ground and hit him with it?"

Ben nodded. "Threw it at him, most likely. You said she had a bit of a temper and liked to throw things when she was upset? Well, it looks like Gazza had really upset her, then he made it worse by walking away from her. Good lesson that – never turn your back on an angry woman!" he added with a sly look at the DI, which she ignored. "Interesting that the prints are along the side," he continued. "If you pick a bottle up intending to use it as a weapon, most people would grab it round the neck. I think she just snatched up the first thing she saw and threw it. Perhaps didn't seriously intend to hit him."

"We've still got the really important question to answer, though. Who killed Cobden?" Wheeler noticed the self-satisfied look on Ben's face. "So you're going to tell me that as well?"

"Yes Ma'am! Branden killed her."

"Branden!" she shook her head. "How does that work, Drummond? You've just established that he was unconscious before she was killed."

"Not unconscious. Just stunned," Ben said. "Here's my scenario. The bottle hits him, he goes down on hands and knees, blood pouring out of him. She sees what she's done, and runs over to help him. He's only semi-conscious. Confused. And he feels someone grabbing at him. He's been attacked, he defends himself. Lashes out wildly. She's only a little slip of a girl, no weight to her, and she's off-balance, leaning over him. She goes flying when he hits her, topples down into the ditch. Lands on her head and..." he shrugged.

DI Wheeler thought it over, and nodded slowly. "It fits the facts. He might not even have known he did it. Or if he did, with his record he wouldn't want to admit it. But it looks like a tragic accident, not murder."

"You could try for a manslaughter charge," Ben suggested.

"Maybe. I'll talk to CPS about that. OK. Good work, Drummond, and I want your Scene Report on my desk before you finish tonight."

Ben met her gaze. "You got it, doll!" he growled in his best transatlantic accent.

She stiffened and glared at him. Then just as Ben was bracing himself for a furious tongue lashing, she sighed and shook her head. "You know what, Drummond? You'll outlive us all."

It was rare that anything surprised Ben, but Helen Wheeler had the satisfaction of seeing his jaw drop.

"What's that supposed to mean?" he asked belligerently.

"You're too bloody cantankerous to die," she told him as she turned to go.

Ben watched her disappear down the path. "Too bloody cantankerous to die," he muttered. A grin spread slowly across his face. "She says the nicest things!"

He set about packing up his equipment, wondering if Wheeler would have fitted into 1930's New York.

DI Wheeler's words proved to be unexpectedly ironic. Just a few weeks after she said them, Ben Drummond was dead. Murdered – and (although she never knew it) it was his attitude that helped him on his way...

This short passage forms the prologue to my crime novel, 'Can of Worms'.

Can of Worms

PROLOGUE

Someone once told Ben Drummond that he was 'too bloody cantankerous to die'. It wasn't meant as a compliment but Ben, being Ben, took it that way. Ironic, really, since it was his sheer cussedness, his awkward, obstructive, cantankerous nature that would kill him. That and a nine millimetre bullet.

Standing at the far end of the cavernous duty garage, Ben felt even more belligerent than usual. He'd been stuck here doing cars all day, and Ben hated doing cars. Some Scenes Of Crime Officers – SOCOs - liked cars. There was a lot of shiny metal and glass to take fingerprints, there were often cig ends in the ashtray, or bottles under the seats. There was a good chance of bringing something back if you went and did some cars.

Ben didn't give a shit about bringing anything back – not for a crappy little stolen car job. Twenty-five years he'd been in the job, and he shouldn't be spending his time on piddling small stuff. In Ben's not very humble opinion, anything less than an aggravated burglary was a waste of his time and experience. But Slippery Mick had come over all officious that morning, and started on about sharing jobs out equally. So Ben was here doing cars, while kids with ten minutes in the job were on burglaries and assaults. Stuck in a damp, cold, badly lit garage, bugger all good for any sort of proper forensic exam anyway, on a damp, cold, badly lit day at the arse-end of October, looking at his sixth car of the shift. And this one wasn't going to lift his mood either, because it was a burnt out wreck. Waste of time, the dimwit PC who had the case shouldn't even have requested scenes of crime.

Unless, perhaps, this was something a bit special? Involved in something serious perhaps – kidnapping, armed robbery? Please, at least a GBH! With a flicker of interest, Ben looked through his paperwork, dug out the incident log, and swore. Just a bloody Taken Without Owners Consent. Bunch of kids had TWOC'd it for a joy ride, torched it for fun. The owner hadn't even reported it until it had already been put out by the Fire Brigade. It was that important.

Well, he wasn't going to waste any time on this one. Not even worth getting his kit out for.

Ben dumped his file on the fire-blackened bonnet, began scribbling on a report form. Ten minutes, he thought, then back to the station for a cuppa and maybe a sausage cob.

Behind him, there were footsteps on the damp concrete, which he ignored. Garage staff, he presumed. Probably brought another car in. Well, if they were thinking of asking him to do it before he left they'd think again bloody damn quick.

'Hum – make, Vauxhall Cavalier.' Ben frequently muttered to himself whilst working. 'Condition – severe fire damage, engine and passenger compartment, all windows out...'

'That's my car.'

Scowling, Ben put his pen down and turned round. The man standing a few yards away was hard to make out. The random failures of the strip lighting had left him in a pool of shadow, back lit by the bright halogens further down.

'What?' Ben growled.

'Are you Police?'

'Scenes of Crime Officer. And this is a forensic examination area. Not open to the public. Garage office is over the other side.'

The man stepped a bit closer, more into what light there was. Ben saw a dark beard, chunky dark coat, eyes shadowed by a baseball cap. 'That's my car there.'

'I'm nearly finished with it. Go over to the garage office, you can sort things out with them.'

'Did you find anything in the car?' The man spoke sharply, demanding an answer.

Ben almost smiled. He loved the chance to be truculent, obstructive, and downright rude if possible.

'Like I told you, this is a forensic examination area. Contact the OIC if you've got any questions. That's the Officer In Charge of the case. Now bugger off!'

The man had kept his hands in his pockets, seemingly casual, but there was no doubting the aggression in his voice or in the way he leaned forward as he spoke.

'Tell me what you've found in my car!'

And for a brief moment, Ben was tempted to say 'Sod all mate. Sorry, it's a negative.' But that would have gone against a lifetime's habit, and instead he snapped back 'Can't tell you that. Police business. Now piss off out of it!' And for the first time that day, he felt almost happy. He was staring straight at the man, glaring in joyful fury, and so was barely aware of the hand that came out of the pocket, or of what it was holding, or of the muffled thud.

But he felt the massive impact in his chest, the tremendously powerful blow that flung him back against the scorched metal of the car. Flung him back and also spun him round, so that he was grasping at the roof, trying to pull himself up, but he had no strength left, none in his arms, none in his legs, and he couldn't stop himself slipping to the floor. He thought of his radio, but he couldn't move to reach it, and already it was very dark, even darker than normal.

And then it was utter black, and Ben Drummond hadn't even had time to realise what had happened.

The shot seemed to echo for a long time, the acoustics of metal walls and concrete floor extending its lifetime beyond the normal. The man with the gun stood listening while they faded – not looking at the body, but at the entrance to the garage. He did not expect interruption from the garage staff, who were watching telly in their portacabin on the other side of the yard. However, just in case, he looked and listened for a while longer, with his pistol hanging casually from his hand.

Finally satisfied that there would be no interruptions, he slipped it back into his pocket, and turned to the body, slumped face down on the dirty concrete.

He had certain business to conduct here, business made more difficult by Ben Drummond's intransigence. Which, in the man's mind, was reason enough to shoot him. Even now, the matter did not go as well as hoped, and he swore several times in frustration. But he was a practical person, and did not linger pointlessly. When he had done as much as could reasonably be done, under the circumstances, he left. The whole thing was something of an irritation, especially as his intervention now seemed unnecessary. But at least he'd made sure if it. It might not have been the best solution, or the ideal outcome, but it had been dealt with quickly, and on the whole, satisfactorily. He took some pleasure in having tied up all the loose ends.

In the garage, nothing moved. Even the pool of blood from beneath the body had stopped spreading. In the poor lighting it was hardly distinguishable from the oil stains nearby as it slowly congealed on the wet concrete.

The rest of the novel concerns one of Ben's colleagues, Marcie Kelshaw, and her dogged hunt for Ben's killer. It's available as a Kindle e-book or a paperback.

The fourth story in this collection takes place post 'Can of Worms'.

Barry Sutter is a Scenes of Crime Officer with a big problem. He's accepted some favours from the wrong sort of person. And now they want payback - which could cost Baz his job and his freedom.

But if he doesn't deliver, it could cost him his life.

A Scene Of Crimes.

In my experience, those who beg for mercy seldom deserve it. In spite of which, I was begging.

"Please – I'm sorry – I'll do it..."

Kincaide continued to push my head against the wall with the muzzle of his gun. He didn't seem inclined towards mercy, deserved or not.

"It's just not that easy..." I continued. Despising the desperate whine in my voice.

"Not easy? All I asked you to do, jerk, was to be in a certain place at a certain time. And you weren't there, were you?"

'Jerk' is what Kincaide calls people he's pissed with. He seemed very pissed with me.

"I got called to a job, urgent, aggravated burglary...." Gabbling. Kincaide talked right over me.

"You kept me waiting, jerk. Three *bloody* hours.....I'm a busy man. I don't like to be kept waiting."

"I – I'm sorry" I said again. "Please – don't .."

"Don't what?" Kincaide leaned on my head, via his pistol. "Don't shoot? Is that what you're asking me, jerk?"

I sobbed. I couldn't help it. It slipped out. Something else was slipping out: I could feel it running down my leg. Kincaide wrinkled his nose.

"You need a shower, Baz."

Actually, I prefer 'Barry' to 'Baz', but I let it pass. It was, after all, a clear improvement on 'jerk.

"So," he continued, "since you're sorry, and since you're asking me nicely, I'll give you one more chance. You go and have your shower, then get out there and get this sorted, alright?"

"Yes, yes, of course, I'll be right on it...."

Kincaide stepped back, handing the gun to one of the big lads he'd brought with him and took out a cigar. With the pressure on my head released, I nearly fell over.

"Two hours, Baz. Be at that address, with your van and all your clever forensic bits and pieces, in two hours. You won't keep me waiting again, will you?"

He didn't say 'Or I'll be back.' He didn't need to. He just stood there smiling gently, puffing on his cigar and watching me struggle to hold myself up against the wall.

Smart suit, wavy grey hair, perfectly groomed – Kincaide looked like a respectable businessman, pillar of the community, everyone's favourite uncle. Until you saw the hardness in his eyes, and realised that this man would walk right through you to get what he wanted.

"Right, then, gentlemen," he said to the two big lads. "We'll be on our way. Mr Sutter has business to attend to." They followed him out, leaving me with my problems.

The first problem was the shaking hands. A stiff drink helped deal with that. In any case, it wasn't really a serious concern. The natural result of adrenaline rush, which in turn was entirely due to how angry I was. For that slick bastard to come in and humiliate me in my own home! Of course I was angry.

And so scared that I'd pissed myself, of course. But for the sake of my remaining shreds of self respect, I pushed that thought aside and went for a shower, as suggested.

The clock was ticking. Ten hundred hours. I had an hour and a half left to Kincaid's deadline, as I slipped behind the wheel of my car. Fifteen minutes to Ash Hill nick, this time of day.

On the way, I thought about my other problems, which could be summed up as Kincaide.

I couldn't remember when we'd first met. Some party, I think, shortly after I'd moved here. Nothing sinister about him then – just a pleasant, affable man, very interested in my job as a Scenes of Crime officer. Nothing unusual about that. Since CSI got popular on TV, everybody's interested in it.

So he liked to talk, and he'd buy the drinks, and there was no harm in sharing a little gossip and some funny stories. Besides, he could be helpful. Having some money trouble? Well – you know – bad investments, divorce, and still got kids to pay for...

No problem. Kincaide knew people; he could talk to a few friends. Interest free loan? Certainly! Pay it back when you can, no rush. Bit of a dump you're living in? He could help with that.

And before long, I was into him for twenty thousand, at least. And the questions became a bit more probing. Who's running this investigation? Did they find anything at that scene?

Of course, I pointed out that there were some things I really shouldn't talk about. This was when I first saw the friendly mask slip a little. He made mention of the Professional Standards Unit, and how interested they might be in how I could afford my house and my car and so on.

I reached the station at ten-fifteen, but there was no chance of finding a space in the car park at that time of day, so I pulled in to a back street nearby. Walking back added another five minutes, but it avoided any awkward questions from people who might recognise my car. Five hours early for a shift wasn't exactly normal behaviour.

I slipped in through the back doors, and made my way cautiously down to the SOCO office. No one about, fortunately. I'd counted on the duty shift being all out and about fighting crime, but there was always the possibility of someone staying in to fight the paperwork instead.

The downside was that most of the vans were out as well. I checked on the status board, and found that the only vehicle still available was the brand-new Peugeot. Our resident Senior had had it specially equipped for major crime scenes, and had informed everyone that it was not to be used without his express permission.

I pocketed the keys without a moment's hesitation. With any luck I'd have it back before it was missed. If not – well, I had bigger things to concern myself with. And at least I knew it was fully stocked, since it hardly ever got used.

Ten minutes later, I was heading out of the gates again. An hour to go. Should make it easily, I thought, but my palms were still sweatier than a cold March day called for.

Kincaide hadn't stopped with requests for information. Once he'd had made my situation clear, the demands increased.

"Baz – there's been a burglary at Worrington Heights. Go and do the examination. *Don't* find anything."

"Baz – about that car from the armed robbery. One of your colleagues found a glove. Make sure that it goes missing."

The latest had been a face to face meeting where he passed me a strip of bloodstained cloth. "Next burglary you go to, Baz, be sure and find this at the scene."

I'd raised a weak objection. "But that's falsifying evidence!"

The mask had slipped a little more then, and I hadn't liked what I saw. "Listen, Jerk. I need a favour doing, and you owe me a lot of favours. Don't piss me about. Ever."

That, I'd come to realise, was the nature of Kincaide's business. He did favours, he collected favours. He brokered information, he made arrangements, he sorted out problems. In return, he expected the same back – favours done, arrangements made, problems solved. And of course, he also skimmed a little profit off the top. All very low key. He never got his hands dirty, never stepped out of the shadows. I'd made discrete enquiries, and CID didn't even have him on their radar. Nobody knew where he lived, where he came from, who he really was.

But he knew a lot about everyone else, and that knowledge was power.

The address he'd given me was on the edge of town, a slightly run-down industrial area. Warehousing, storage facilities, some small businesses. I found the place at the end of a side street. A featureless block of concrete, with a faded sign outside – something about 'Import / Export'. There was some activity at the far end, with fork lifts loading or unloading an artic trailer, but near the gates there was only one of Kincaide's big lads. He waved me in through a cavernous doorway. I pulled up inside, next to Kincaide's Merc, and heard the roller shutter rumbling down behind me.

Not a nice feeling. Not with Kincaide standing by his car, giving me a hostile stare.

This morning had been the first time he'd really shown his violent streak. Normally he preferred low-key threats. Hints, suggestions, friendly warnings. Mind you, when he'd called me in the middle of yesterday evenings shift, and told me to get over at once, he hadn't sounded low key. I'd tried to explain then that I had another commitment – knowing that it wouldn't go down well – but until he'd burst into my house and stuck a gun against my skull, I hadn't realised what he was capable of.

This whole thing was a long way from his normal M.O. Something had got him very pissed, and somehow I was involved. It didn't bode well.

For a moment the thought crossed my mind that I could put the van in gear and drive straight over him. But murder wasn't a decision to make on the spur of the moment. Plus which the big lads, probably armed, were standing around, and the exit was closed. I switched off the engine and climbed out.

"Finally." Kincaide grunted, though I had at least twenty minutes left. "Over here."

I followed him towards a side door.

"They got in here," he announced. "Forced the roller shutter, forced the fire escape door. Then went across to those stairs."

"Hang on a minute." I said slowly. "What's this – a crime scene?"

"Of course it's a bloody crime scene." Kincaide snapped. "What the hell do you think I wanted a SOCO for – cook my dinner? Someone broke in here. I want to know who. You're going to find out for me."

The first thing that I nearly said was "Have you reported it?" Which would have been really stupid, and Kincaide was clearly not in the mood for stupid. So I swallowed that, and crunched my mental gears into crime scene examination mode.

"Um – when did it happen?"

'Night before last. Sometime between midnight and seven."

I thought back. It had rained heavily since then, there probably wouldn't be much to find outside, but I'd better do a proper job. "Let's see that door then..." I fetched my kit from the van and got to work.

It didn't take more than a glance to confirm that the outside surfaces were 'no forensic value'. Apart from the weather, the worn metal, flaking paint and rough wood weren't surfaces that would take a fingerprint. All I could say was that from the size and shape of the tool marks, the offenders had probably used a crowbar. Which wasn't a lot of good unless you actually had a suspect with a crowbar in their possession.

I tried to explain that to Kincaide. The reaction was unfavourable.

"Baz, you really are a jerk. You really don't get it, do you?"

I wasn't sure how to answer that. It seemed that it was a rhetorical question in any case. Instead of waiting for an answer, the lads dragged me inside, pushed me against the wall, and handed Kincaide the gun again. This time he just showed it to me. That was more than sufficient – I could still remember how it felt.

"Some little arsehole has done this place over." Kincaide continued. "And I want to know who, so I can rip their balls off. Slowly." Something about his demeanour suggested that this was not a figure of speech. "Your job, jerk, is to get me a name. I'm not interested in hearing what you don't know and what you can't do. Just get me a name. Do you understand now?"

I nodded, carefully. The lads let me go, but I stayed leaning against the wall. Thankfully, I'd managed not to piss myself this time, which was some sort of progress. Very important, I felt, to focus on the positives. I looked round in hope of finding another one.

This end of the warehouse was walled off from the working section, and was empty apart from the two vehicles. However, it had seen regular use in the past: the concrete floor was well marked with tyre tracks and partial footprints in the dust. No point in wasting my time with those, however. Kincaide wanted a name, which meant fingerprints or DNA.

"You say they went up those stairs?" I asked. Metal stairs, leading to a door high up in the walled section. "And through that door?" Kincaide nodded. "Any alarms?"

"The whole warehouse is on one system." He answered, frowning. For once, not at me. "Alarm box outside, though. The bastards drilled a hole in it and filled it with that spray foam stuff."

"Wall cavity insulation?"

"Yeah, that. When it hardened, it jammed the bell, bollixed the lot".

"That's a pretty old technique." I commented. "I haven't seen it done for a while."

"Old alarm system." Kincaide replied shortly. "I'll be talking to someone about that. Are you going to examine those stairs or not?"

The handrail was worn metal, not the best surface for fingerprints, but I brushed some aluminium powder over it anyway. Nothing showed but a few smudges. I carried on up to the door.

Wooden door. Rough wood, matt paint, nothing that would take a fingerprint. Same tool marks as before. The lock had been wrenched out and the frame split. I pulled it open and went in.

Originally this would have been the office area. But it had had a makeover. The creamy carpet was so thick that I nearly tripped, and the room had been furnished by someone with taste and no budgetary constraints.

Deep leather chairs, of a shade to match the carpet. A coffee table in wood and glass, several impressive looking pictures on the walls.

An empty set of brackets on another wall, where a big plasma TV had probably been.

The place had been comprehensively trashed. Drawers emptied, furniture pulled around and turned over. I walked through, stepping carefully over smashed ornaments.

Through the door beyond was a dining room, with a huge table of beautifully polished wood. Mahogany, I thought. To one side was a gleaming kitchen, with a walk-in pantry, on the other an office. Two big bedrooms and a good-sized bathroom completed the accommodation. All furnished and decorated to the same high standard, all thoroughly and messily searched.

"Your place?" I asked Kincaide.

He gave me a very cold look.

"I need to know," I explained carefully. "If you live here, your fingerprints will be here. You don't want me recovering those. I need to know who's been here and touched things, legitimately that is."

He nodded slowly. "Yes, this is my place. One of them. I was last here three nights ago. But since then it's been thoroughly cleaned. It gets cleaned every day. Completely. Everything washed up or wiped down. And no, the cleaners would not have left any of their prints. I've already talked to them."

I felt a chill of apprehension for the cleaners. They would have been Kincaide's first suspects. "So anything I find...?"

"Yeah. Whatever you get, it's the little shits who did this."

I wasn't entirely convinced, since even the most thorough cleaning can leave evidence behind. But this wasn't the time to mention it. "What did they take?"

"Everything. Every damn thing they could lift... TV's, cash, jewellery, laptop from the office."

I got to work, examining surfaces for DNA traces, dusting all likely objects for prints. Kincaide and his men watched every move.

I was beginning to get very worried. If I didn't find anything, Kincaide's displeasure might be fatal. I'd seen that gun at close quarters twice already, and I had a nasty feeling that the next time would be a close encounter of the final kind.

But even if I did find something, I might not be safe. Kincaide was a man who liked his secrets, and now I knew some of them. I knew where he lived, or sometimes lived. I knew that his minders carried guns, and that he didn't mind using one himself. That aptitude for violence hadn't developed overnight. The man had a past, I guessed, probably a record somewhere. He'd put that behind him, moved on to better things... but I now knew about it. I had seen him out of the shadows.

Which meant that he could no longer hold Professional Standards over me. He wouldn't want me spilling my guts to them.

However this worked out, I realised, I was in serious trouble. The only reason Kincaide hadn't already blown my skull open was that he still had a use for me. Mercy didn't come into it.

I was powdering a mirrored wardrobe door in the master bedroom when I completed that disturbing thought. Normally, surfaces like that are covered with marks. In the right environment, fingerprints can linger for weeks, even months, and I would expect to find smudged or partial traces from every time the doors had been opened. But the cleaners were as thorough as Kincaide had said, and the surface was pristine.

Except at one point, where four distinct finger shapes appeared, almost magically, as I passed the brush over them.

"There!" Kincaide shouted triumphantly.

"Yes, looks like it." I agreed. But I'd already seen the fabric marks. Regular, parallel lines inside the finger shapes. Whoever had had their fingers on the mirror had been wearing gloves.

I carefully built up the marks with a bit more powder, doing my best to stay between them and Kinkaide as I did so. Let him think that I'd got real fingerprints. It might just get me out of here. And then? I wasn't sure. Perhaps I'd go to Professional Standards. It would cost me my career and probably send me to prison, but my life expectancy would improve.

Or not. Grassing Kincaide up would confirm me on his shit list, which could quickly turn into a hit list. With his knowledge and connections, it was quite likely that he could avoid any charges brought against him. Whereas If I ended up in the pokey, I'd be dead within a week. I'm sure that Kincaide knew a lot of people in Her Majesty's Prisons.

The marks lifted well, as they should have from that surface, and I sealed them down onto an acetate sheet. "There you are." I told Kincaide, waving the sheet around without letting him see it too closely. "I can send these off to the Fingerprint Bureau later today. I'll slip them in with another job – and if I ask them to rush it, we could have a result tomorrow."

Kincaide smiled. The old, friendly, everybody's-favourite-uncle Kincaide was back. For now.

"Good! Well done, Baz. I knew you wouldn't let me down. And I *will* show my gratitude, don't worry! Now then..." He glanced at his watch. "Now that's sorted, I've got something else to attend to."

"Right then." I said. "I'll just get my kit together."

"Oh, you can stay for a bit, Baz. Finish the job. You've still got the other bedroom and the bathroom to do. Might find something else." He gave me a sharp look. "Not in a hurry to go, are you?"

I was, because I had to get the van back and start my proper shift. But that wasn't what he wanted to hear.

"No, of course not."

"I'm glad to hear that. Because I wouldn't want you to miss anything. After all, if those prints don't get us a name, then I would be quite disappointed. I'm sure you wouldn't want that, would you?"

I shook my head.

"I thought not. Larry – you stay here and see our friend out when he's finished. And get someone in to clean up this mess. I want to be able to stay here again tonight. Come on, Mick. We'll leave them to it."

I returned to my examination and my gloomy thoughts. The glove marks had got me a reprieve, but not a long one. If I didn't turn myself in, it would only be a matter of time – and not much off it – before Kincaide wanted to know what name the supposed fingerprints had produced. And I didn't think he'd accept any excuses either.

Larry had wandered off somewhere, probably on the phone getting the cleaning sorted out. That suited me. It was easier to work without someone peering over my shoulder all the time. Not that there was much more to do. There was nothing to find in the second bedroom except a few more smudgy glove marks. Since I wasn't being observed, I quickly rubbed them out. No point in wasting time with them, I thought despondently. It was clear that whoever had turned Kincaide over was at least bright enough to wear gloves.

Not very bright to do Kincaide's place, of course, but I was pretty certain that they hadn't known what they were getting into. My guess would have been that they'd assumed that these rooms were offices. Probably hoping to get a few laptops, maybe a little petty cash. They must have thought it was all their birthdays come at once when they got into this little treasure trove.

If Kincaide caught up with them, they'd have a different point of view. But at the moment, they were looking pretty safe. And I was getting desperate.

Nothing left but the bathroom. I walked in, switched on the light, and an extractor fan started up. No windows. It was as smart as the rest of the flat, done out with black and silver tiles throughout. Big bath, separate shower, toilet like a small throne.

The burglar's hadn't spent much time in here, though. A few toiletries had been knocked off shelves near the sink. I dusted them, but without much hope, and got the negative result I'd expected. Waste of time, I thought. I'd be better off getting out of here and either going to Professional Standards or making arrangements to leave the country.

There was a large mirror set in the wall above the sink. I glanced at it, wondering if there were any marks worth powdering before I wrapped things up. Switched the mirror light on for a better look, and was surprised when another extractor fan started up with a discreet whine.

Unusual to have a second extractor, I thought. I could see it now, a small grille just above the mirror, between two lights, carefully blended into the decoration.

I also saw an ashtray built into the sink. Custom made. Knowing Kincaide's fondness for cigars, it explained the fan. Obviously, he liked to come in smoking while he smartened himself up, slicked his hair, or whatever. The main extractor wouldn't clear the smoke away quickly enough, so he'd had a second one fitted.

Quite an up-market model as well, not that I'd have expected less. There was a small control panel next to the fan: you could set it for three different speeds, no less. Or you could even reverse it. Why anyone would do that I had no idea. Perhaps Kincaide sometimes liked to feel the wind in his face? More likely it was just a feature added on to show how up-market it was.

I had an amusing thought. Suppose I switched it to blow? Kincaide would come in here with his cigar, switch the light on, and

55

get a face full of smoke and ash.

A petty sort of revenge, but probably all I would get. I really needed Kincaide to suffer something more serious than hot cigar ash up his nose. Though if I was lucky he might choke on it.

I stared at the fan, and then at the ashtray, while an idea took shape. A possibility. A way to perhaps solve all my problems. Perhaps.

Considering how much shit I was in, I had nothing to lose.

A few minutes later, I came out of the bathroom, and found Larry.

"You can tell Mr. Kincaide that we've definitely got them!" I announced proudly, waving an evidence bag full of swabs under his nose. "Smear of blood in the bathroom. Not a lot, but it'll get us a DNA profile."

Actually, it was my blood, but I thought it would help to put Kincaide in a good mood and assure him that I was obeying orders. It worked well enough on Larry, who actually smiled as he escorted me out and back to the van.

I managed to get to Ash Hill just before the start of my shift. I did get caught trying to sneak the van keys back, but bullshitted my way out with a story about checking that it was stocked up in case something big came in that night. That earned me some puzzled looks, since this was not my normal attitude to the job, but it got me off the hook.

As it happened, something big did come in late that night. A fatal fire in a warehouse. A puzzling business - even the Fire Service investigator couldn't be sure what had happened.

"It looks as thought some idiot had converted the office area into a flat." He told me when I arrived. "No planning permission... the old sprinkler system was disconnected, and the place must have been stuffed with flammables. Went up like a torch, spread into the warehouse area. The whole buildings gutted. I don't think there's going to be much for you to do, even when it's cooled down."

He was right. They'd found the body in what had been the bedroom, and with the entire structure in danger of collapse, the examination was cut short on health and safety grounds. Nobody even got close to examining the bathroom, or the fan.

They did manage to get the corpse out for post mortem. Remnants of a brandy glass were found with it, the cracked stem still in hand. The presumption was that the alcohol had been splashed onto the clothing, and was ignited by a cigarette. Or something similar.

The brandy was a bonus. It had helped. But the real killer had been the flaked aluminium fingerprint powder that I'd poured into the fan above the mirror.

Nasty stuff, that. A common ingredient in pyrotechnics, apparently. We had a warning memo a while back, telling us not to use a vacuum cleaner on any powder spills. Because an aerosol of fine aluminium powder is potentially explosive. Only needs a spark to set it off.

Or a burning cigar.

The way I reconstructed it, Kincaide had gone into the bathroom with his cigar alight – just as I'd hoped.

He'd switched on the mirror light, and the fan, set to blow, sent the powder straight into his face. Straight into that glowing cigar tip, burning at over four hundred degrees C. Seven hundred if he was drawing on it.

The aluminium dust ignited. Kincaide jerked backwards, splashing the brandy over him. That went up as well.

Head and upper body ablaze, he staggered out into the bedroom, and collapsed next to the bed. Which caught light, and it spread from there.

I don't know what happened to Larry and Mick. If they were there, they got out fast. Sensible of them. There wasn't much they could have done for Kincaide, anyway.

My colleague who attended the post mortem told me that the (still unidentified) corpse had suffered terrible burns. Not just externally, but in his lungs and nasal passages. Apparently, he had involuntarily inhaled when the fireball exploded round his head. Nasty way to go.

I can't help wondering if Kincaide would have begged for mercy. I can't see it, somehow.

Doesn't matter. He didn't deserve it anyway..

About the Author

Paul began making up stories before he could even write. It turned out to be an unbreakable habit. Since then he's been a seaman, a janitor, an administrator, a missionary and a CSI, but he's always been a story-maker.

He currently writes crime stories, fantasy adventures and science fiction. A lot of his work can be found on Amazon.

He currently lives in the West Midlands, UK, with his wife, three sons, one dog and a variable number of chickens (depending on visits from the local fox).

Read more at yearningblue.weebly.com.

Printed in Poland
by Amazon Fulfillment
Poland Sp. z o.o., Wrocław